The FLASH

RACES THE ROGUES

written by
MATTHEW K. MANNING

illustrated by
ETHEN BEAVERS

STONE ARCH BOOKS
a capstone imprint

DC Super Hero Stories are published by Stone Arch
Books, a Capstone Imprint
1710 Roe Crest Drive
North Mankato, Minnesota 56003
www.mycapstone.com

Summary: THE FLASH is up against four of his
worst Rogues. Barry Allen must think back to his
childhood of growing up alone. He had to fend
for himself back then, and he realizes he'll have
to do the same now.

Editor: Anna Butzer
Art Director: Bob Lentz
Graphic Designer: Hilary Wacholz

STAR37630

Printed in the United States of America.
010058S17

Cataloging-in-Publication Data is available at the
Library of Congress website.
ISBN: 978-1-4965-4633-3 (library binding)
ISBN: 978-1-4965-4637-1 (paperback)
ISBN: 978-1-4965-4649-4 (eBook PDF)

TABLE OF CONTENTS

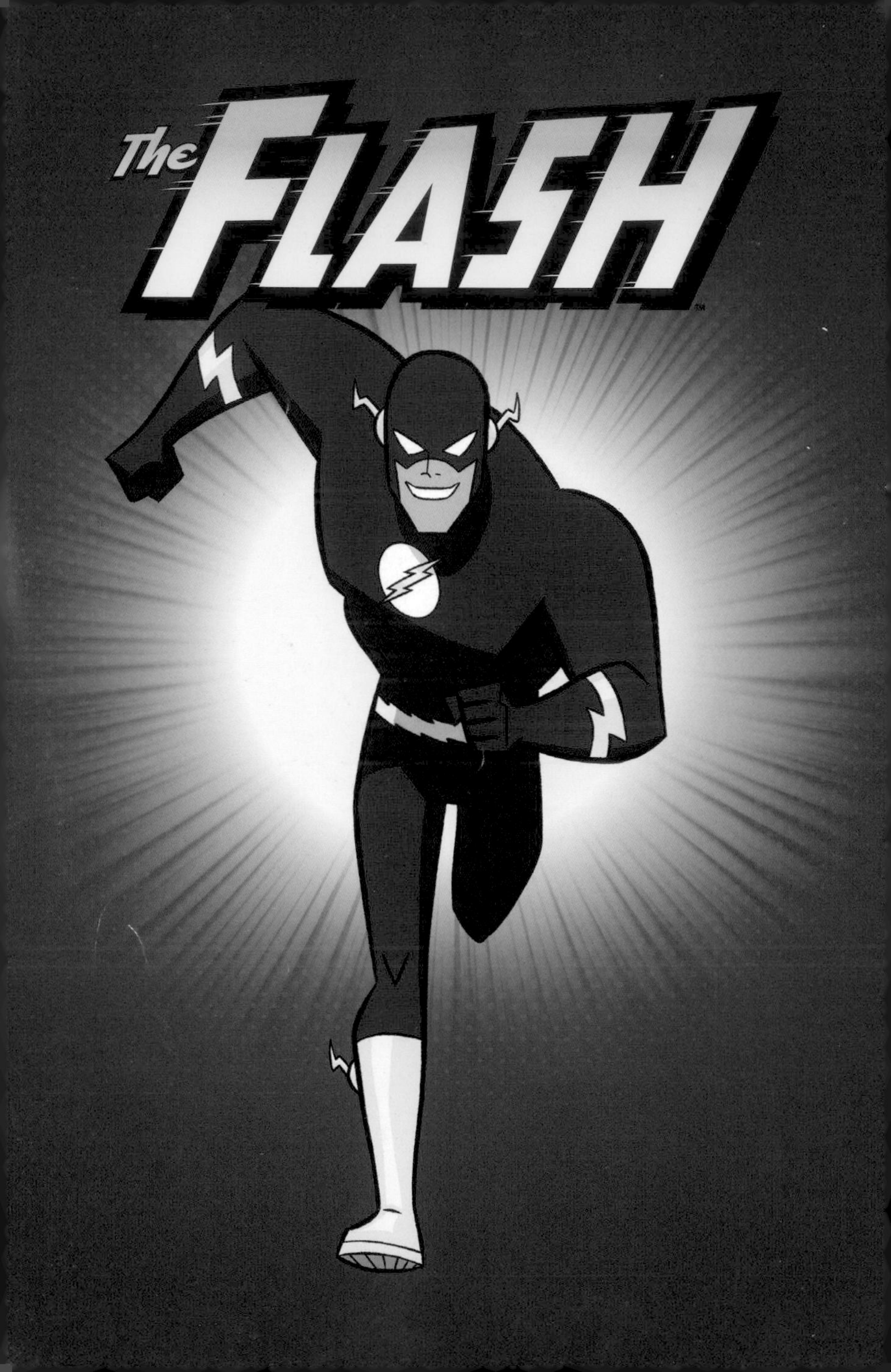
The FLASH

REAL NAME: Bartholomew Henry "Barry" Allen

ROLE: Super hero and forensic scientist

BASE: Central City

HEIGHT: 6'0"

EYES: Blue

HAIR: Blond

ABILITIES: Can move, think, and react at the speed of light. He is able to run long distances without getting tired and heal faster than the average human. Possesses in-depth knowledge of chemistry and criminal psychology.

BACKGROUND: After being covered in chemicals and struck by lightning, forensic scientist Barry Allen became the fastest man alive. He is able to race up buildings, run on water, and create sonic booms. He now protects his hometown of Central City as The Flash.

CHAPTER 1

THE WIND PICKS UP

A sudden gust of wind rips through Central City. Magazines nearly blow off their racks on the newsstands. Men lose their hats. Women hold tight to their handbags. A young boy finds it hard to keep ahold of his newly purchased comic book.

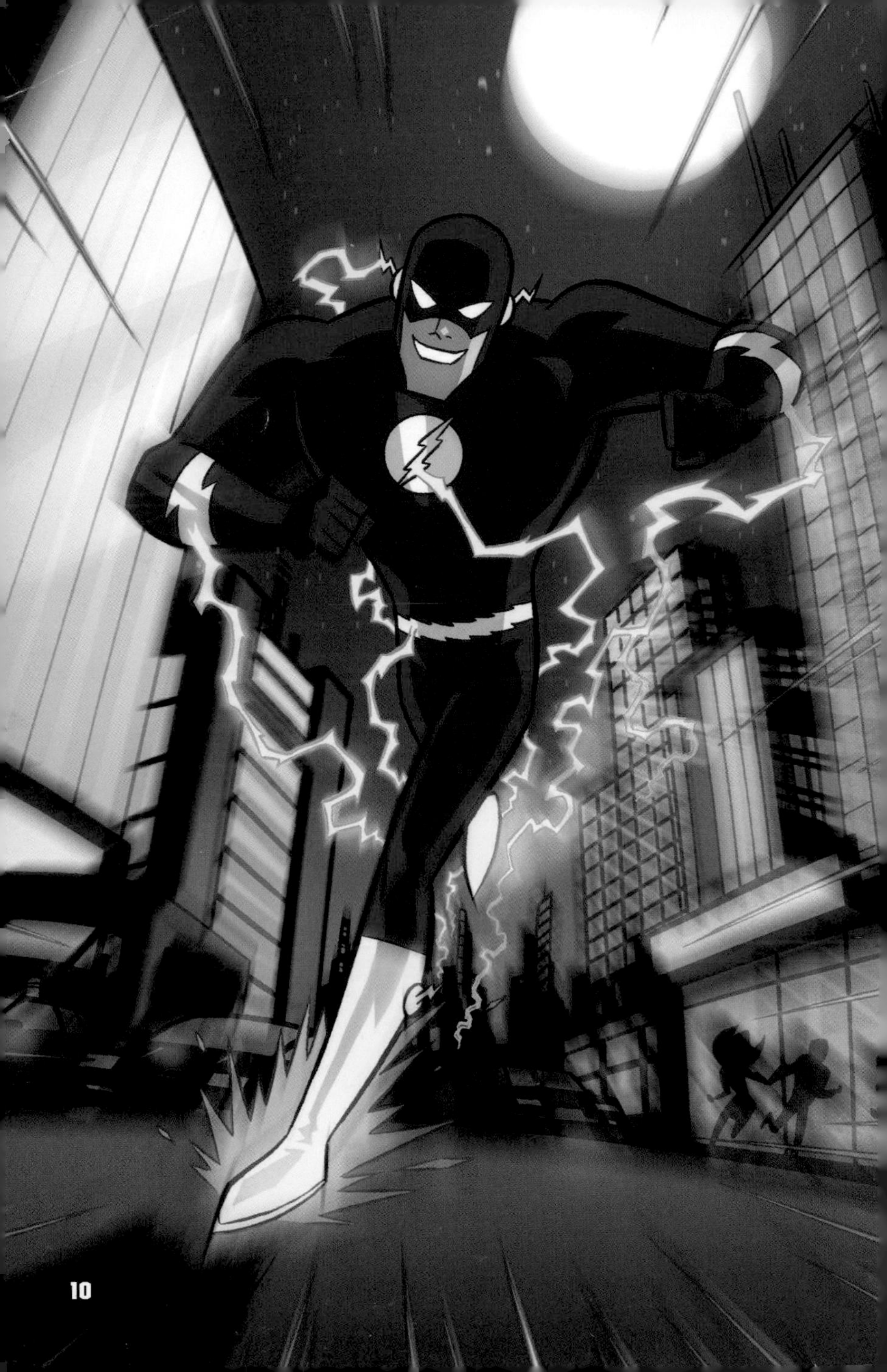

Those with quick reflexes catch a glimpse of someone through the gale.

WHOOSH!

"Did you see that?" asks the hot dog vendor on the corner.

"You bet. And I know only one man who can move like that," replies the customer standing next to the vendor.

To the citizens of Central City, that man looks like a red streak, a crimson blur. But the people of the city know who he is without thinking twice.

He is the Fastest Man Alive.
He is . . . The Flash!

While he spends his days as forensic scientist Barry Allen, The Flash is happiest when he is wearing his brilliant red uniform. Admittedly, his work as a super hero is much more dangerous than his day job. But for The Flash there is nothing better than the wind on his face and the sound barrier booming in his wake.

BZZZZT!

Suddenly, the police radio crackles in The Flash's earpiece. He presses his hand against his ear to hear the emergency call.

"Robbery in progress," says the voice in The Flash's ear. "All available officers to Central Bank and Trust."

"That sounds like my kind of party," The Flash whispers to himself.

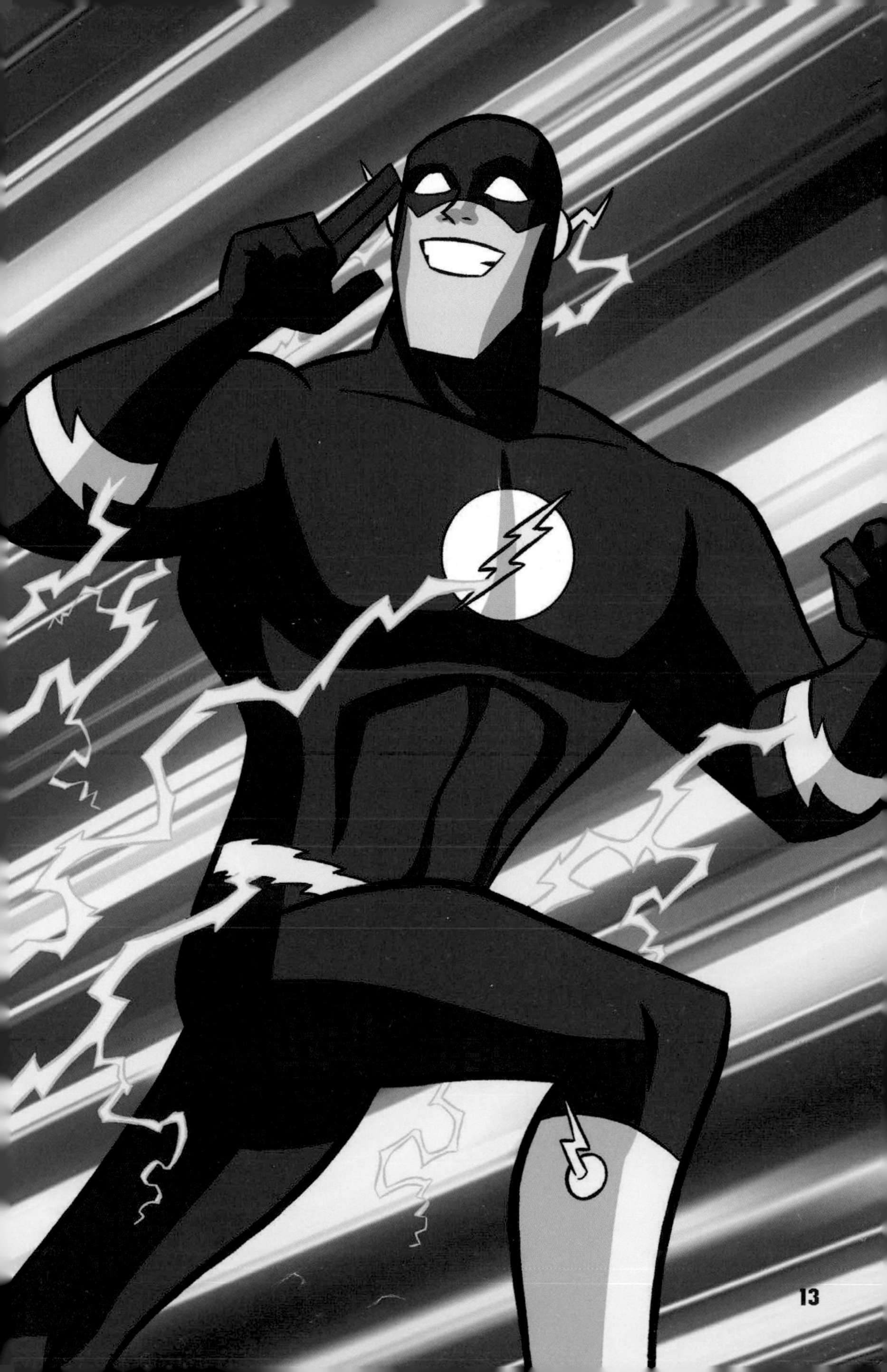

As quick as he can think it, The Flash switches directions. His feet kick dirt and dust into the air behind him. He dashes down a narrow alley to take a shortcut to Central Bank and Trust. The trash cans in the alley spin in place from the rush of wind The Flash creates.

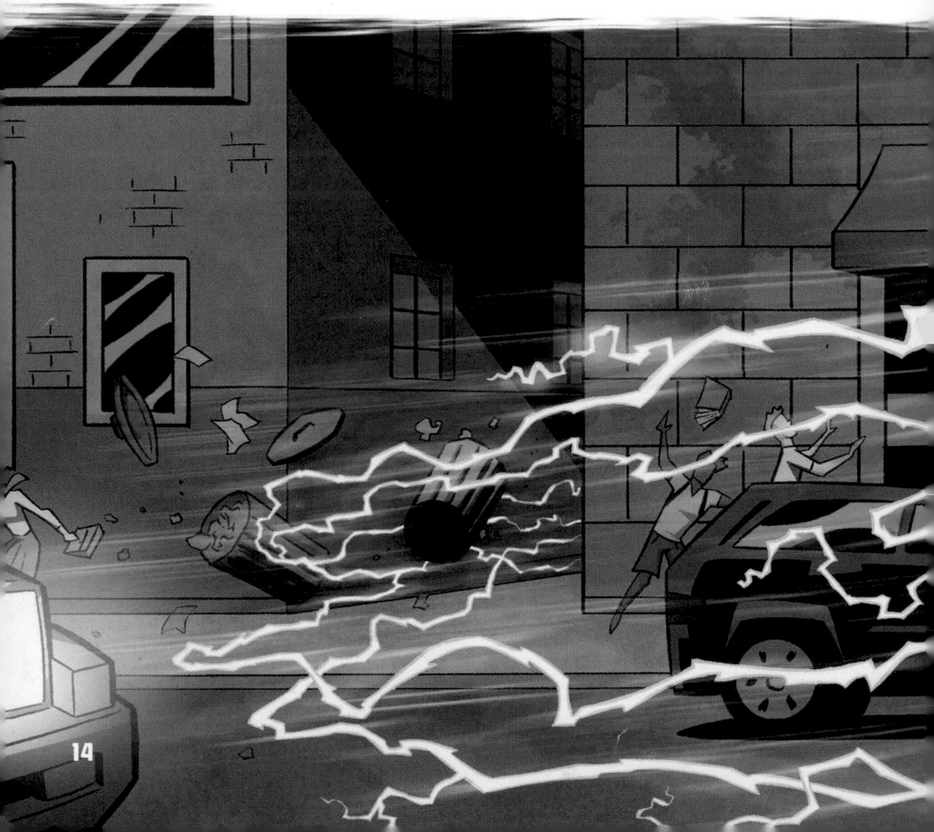

"It's . . . it's the Mirror Master," says the voice on the police's radio frequency. "We need backup on the double."

The hero frowns and picks up speed. The Flash zips in and out of traffic and careens around corners. He can't afford to waste a second. Mirror Master is one of his most dangerous foes.

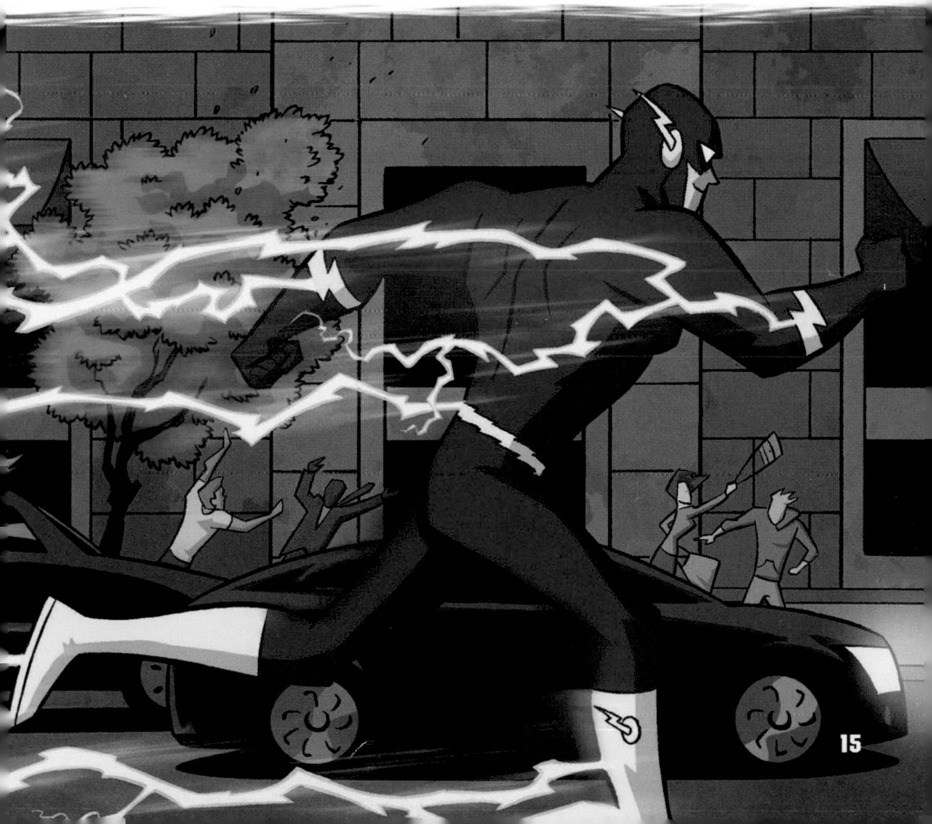

With his mind on his mission, The Flash doesn't notice the patch of ice on the sidewalk in front of him . . . until it's much too late. He loses his balance. Even before his lightning-fast mind can process it, he begins falling to the hard concrete.

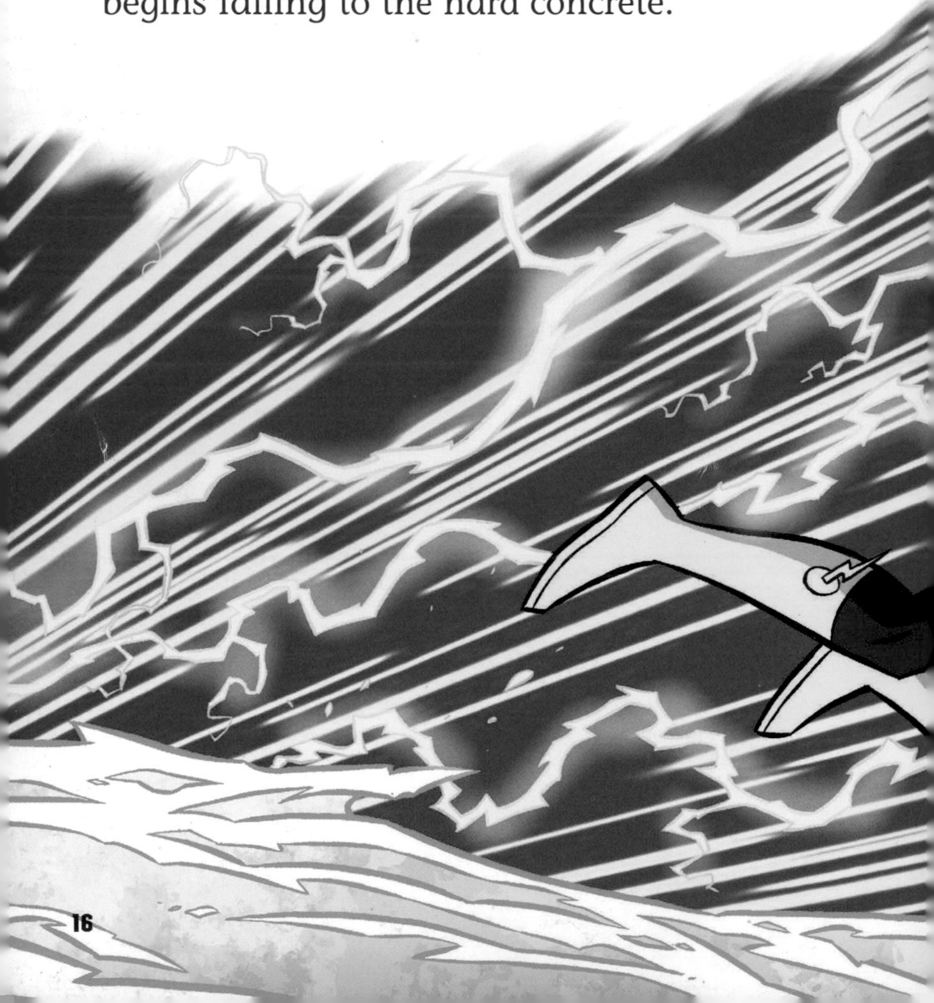

Instinctively, he puts his hands out in front of himself and braces for impact.

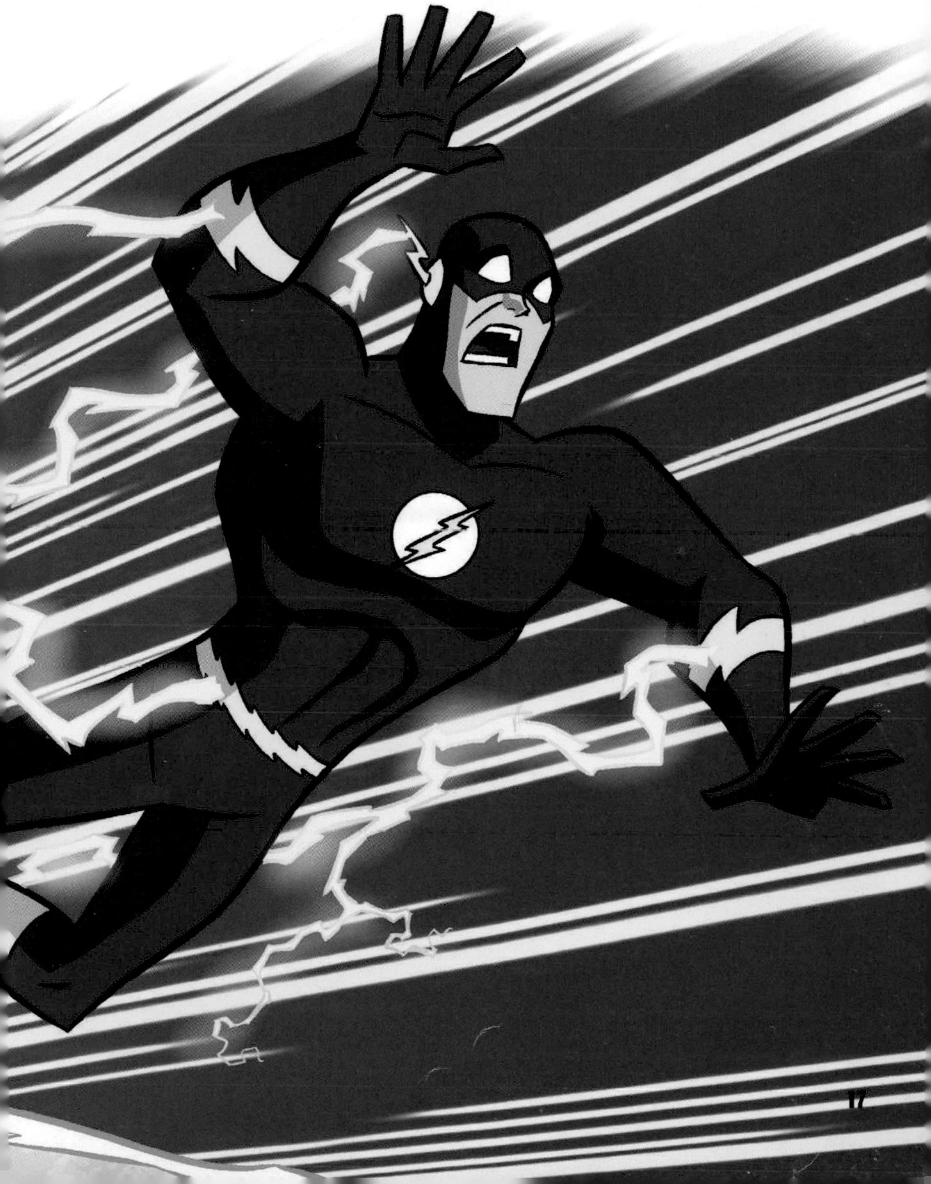

CHAPTER 2

A Cold Front Moves In

It takes the hero only a moment to get back to his feet. But in that moment, The Flash hears a familiar laugh behind him. It belongs to another wicked face from his Rogues Gallery . . . Captain Cold!

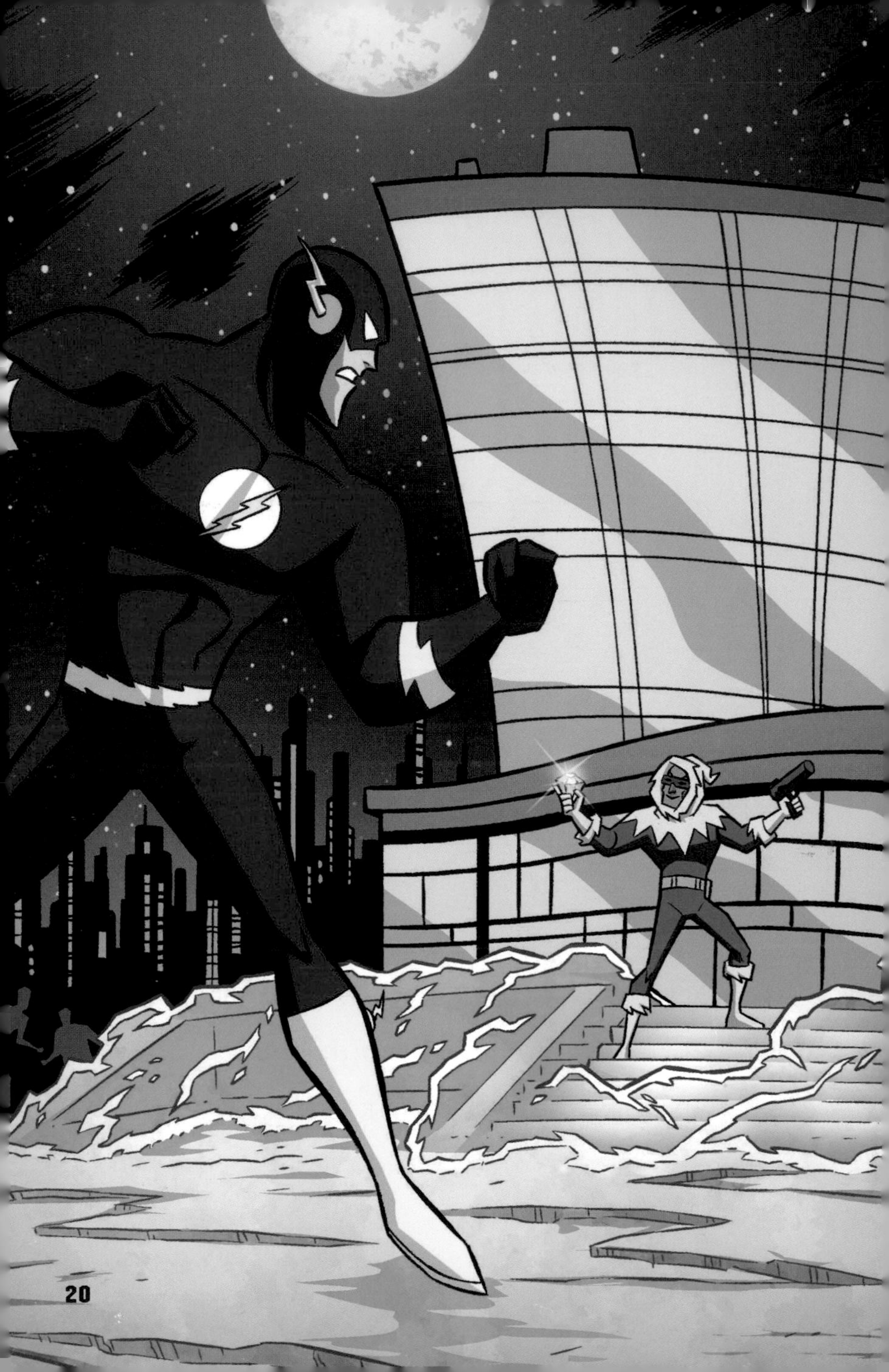

"Don't get up on my account," says the villain. "I'm used to a frigid reception."

"How long have we known each other?" says The Flash as he starts to run toward Captain Cold. "It's been years, right?"

"Yeah, and you still give me the cold shoulder!" the villain says as he raises his specialized cold gun and fires.

"You've had years to work on your material, and you're still making cold puns," The Flash says. The hero dodges the blast with more ease than even he imagined.

Captain Cold opens his mouth to offer another tired comeback, but The Flash isn't listening. The police radio is once again buzzing in his ear.

"Robbery in progress," says the voice. "Corner of 4th and Jackson. It's Heat Wave!"

KRINNG!

"Good grief!" The Flash sighs as he avoids another blast of fast-forming ice. "As if this cold fish wasn't enough. Now I need to deal with a hot head."

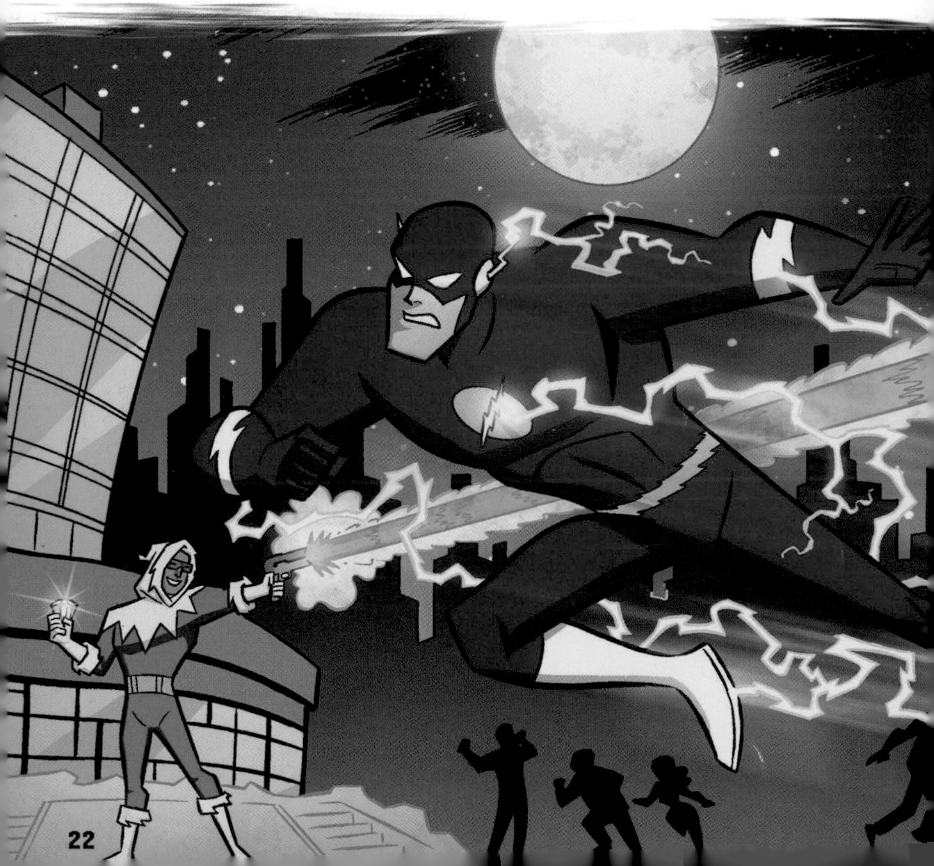

BZZZT!

Just then, the police radio buzzes once more

"Now what?" the Scarlet Speedster mutters. "Don't tell me another villain is on the loose."

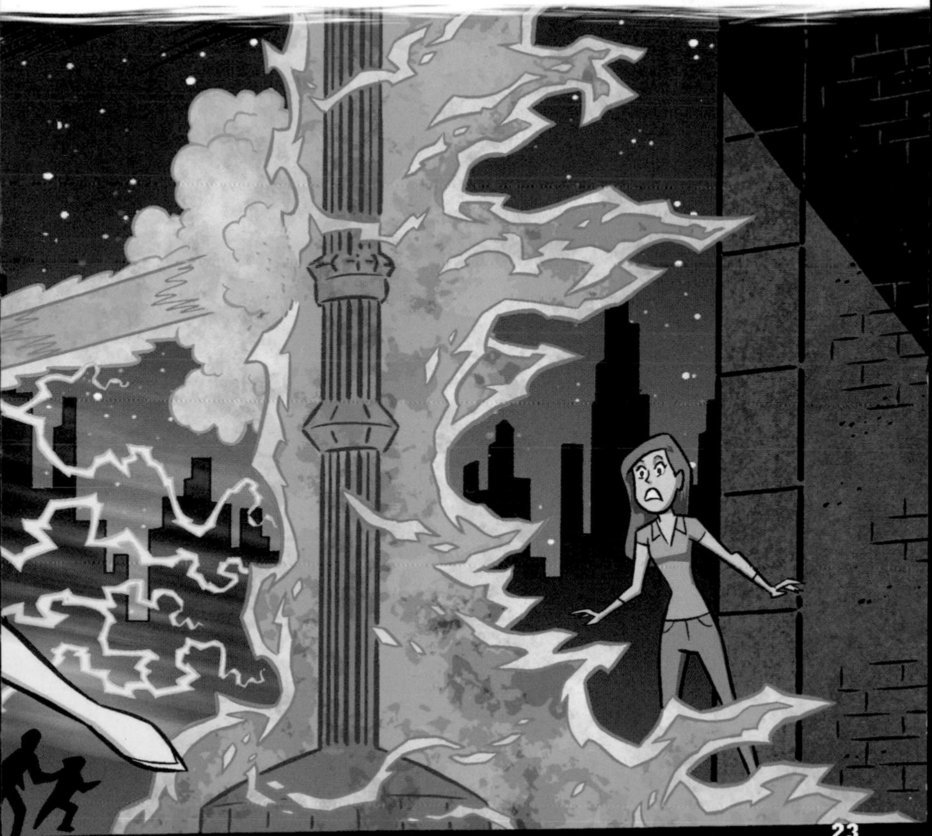

"Weather Wizard spotted," says another voice from the police radio in his cowl. "He's at Highland Plaza stirring up what appears to be a tornado."

"What?" asks The Flash. He didn't mean for it to be out loud. "What's going on today?"

Even the Scarlet Speedster can't be in four places at once. With a thought that moves faster than his legs, The Flash decides to call for backup.

KRINNG!

Before he can place the call, Captain Cold fires his cold gun toward a young girl.

WHOOOSH!

The Flash streaks forward and swoops her out of the path of the icy blast.

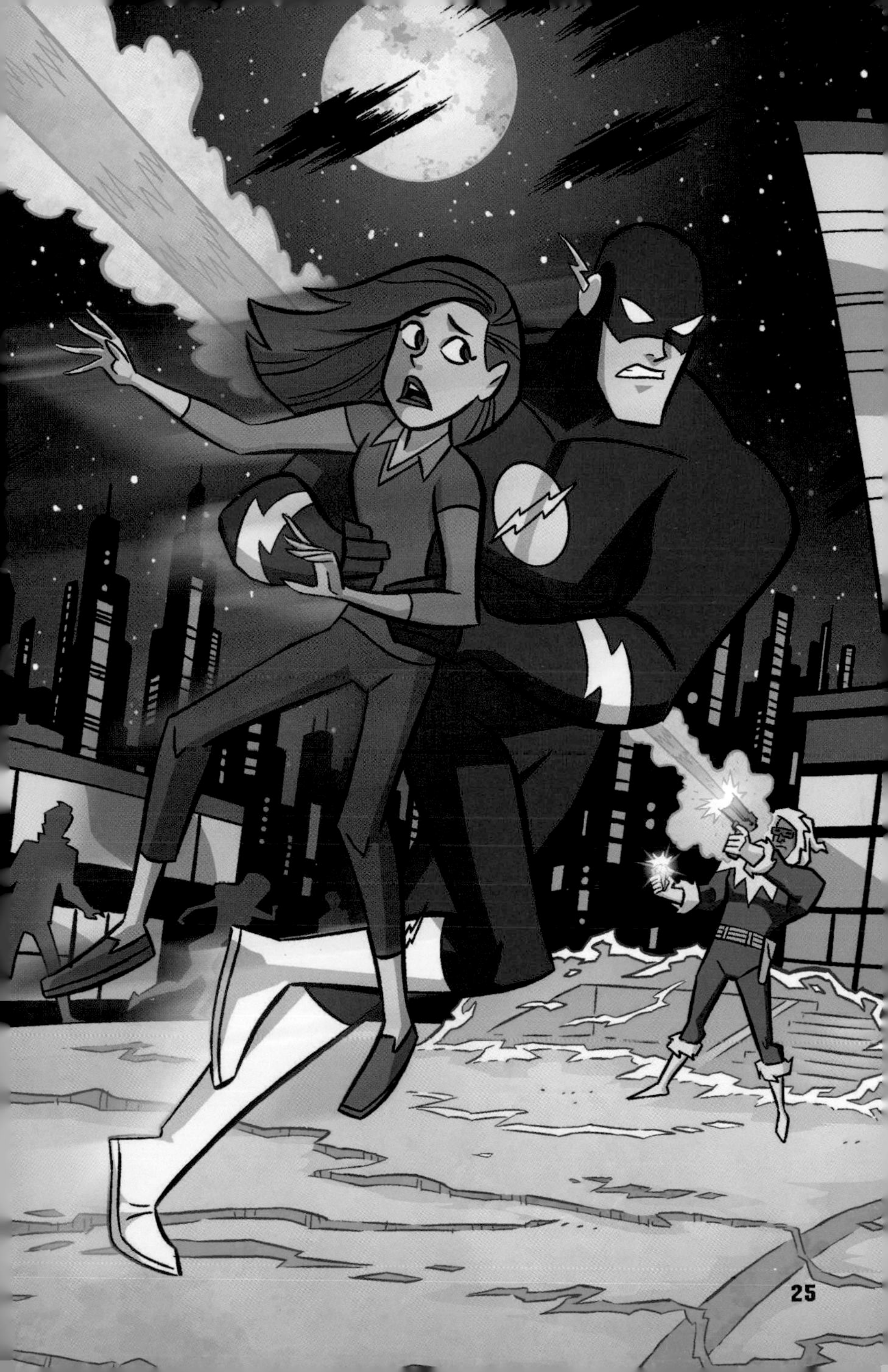

The Flash carries the young onlooker to safety a block away from Captain Cold. The girl hardly has time to thank him with even a smile before The Flash zips away down the street. Then he presses a button on his earpiece.

"Flash to Watchtower," he says. "It's revenge of the Rogues here in Central City! I'm outnumbered by Mirror Master, Captain Cold, Heat Wave, and Weather Wizard. I could really use some backup."

"Green Lantern here. I'm afraid everyone is off-planet at the moment on another mission."

"Huh, well now I just feel left out," The Flash replies.

"I know what you mean," says Green Lantern.

"You're welcome to join my party," The Flash replies.

"Sorry, Barry." Green Lantern says. "I need to stay here at my post. I hope you can figure something out fast."

The Flash smirks and says, "Well that's the only way I know how."

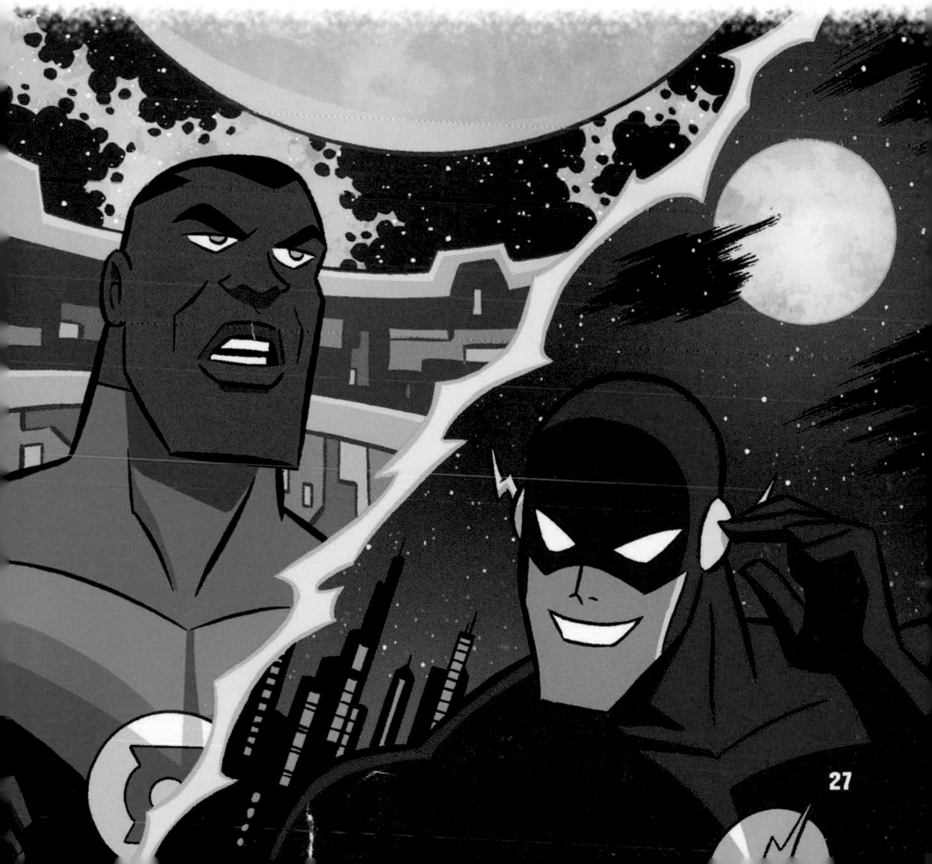

With his fellow super heroes of the Justice League off-planet, there is no help. There is no backup. Against four of his worst Rogues, The Flash is utterly and completely . . . alone.

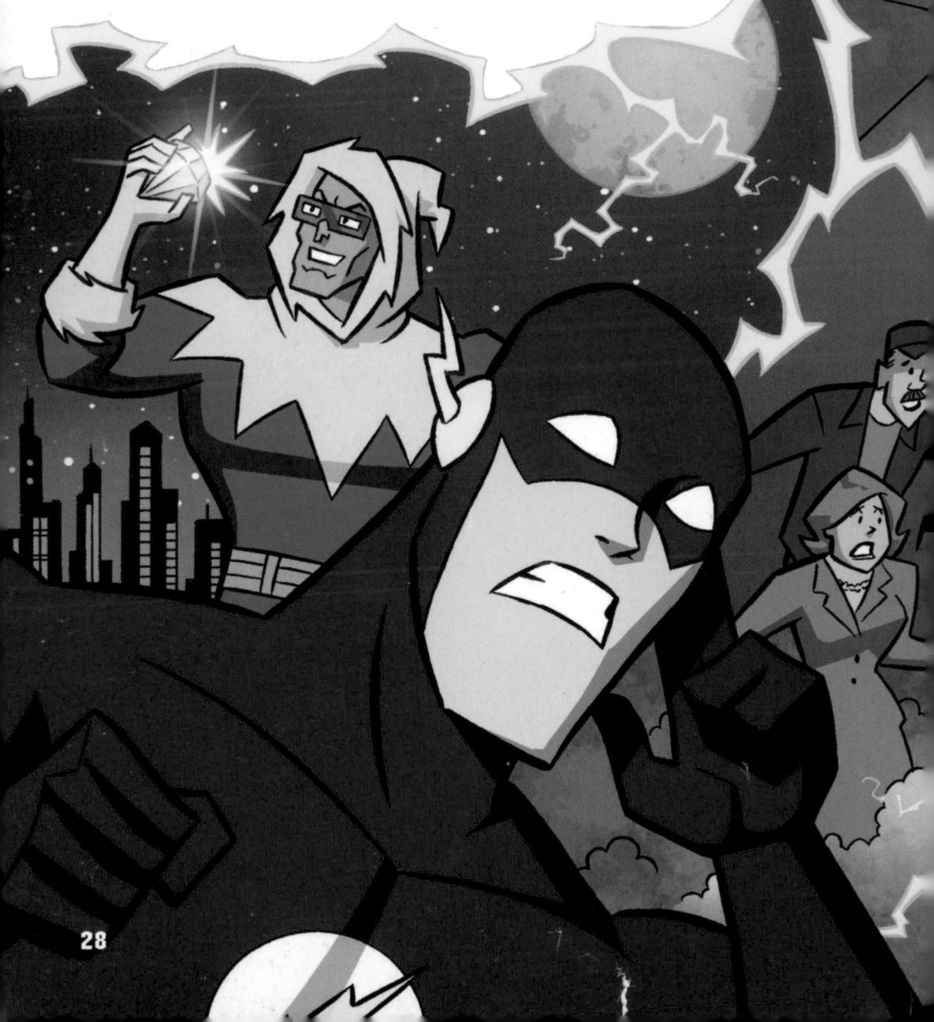

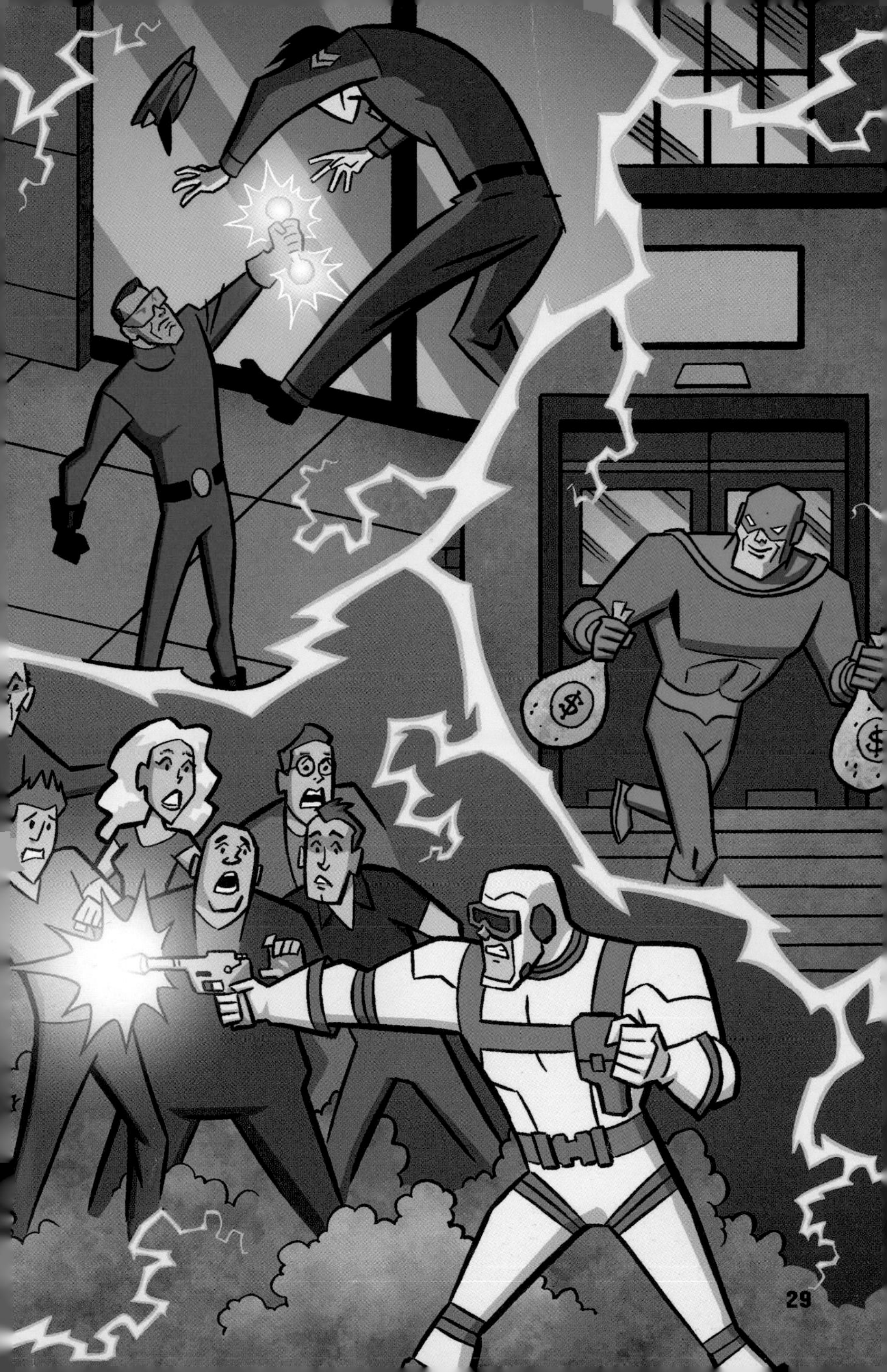

CHAPTER 3

THE GATHERING STORM

It's not the first time that Barry Allen has felt alone. When he was just a young boy, Barry returned from school to find his home had become a crime scene. His mother had been killed.

To make matters worse, the police made a terrible mistake. They believed his father was to blame for the horrible crime. They placed him in handcuffs. Without a word, the police marched his father down the sidewalk. They made sure he didn't hit his head as he was placed inside the police car.

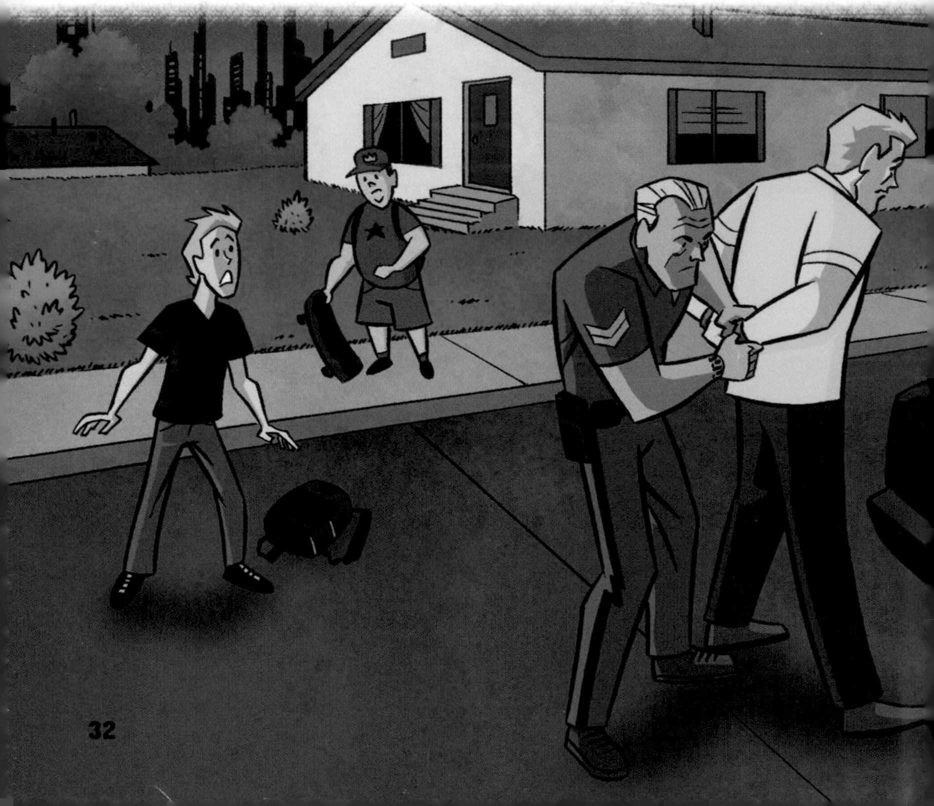

As young Barry Allen looked at his father through the back window of the squad car, he knew one thing for certain. In an instant, his family had been ripped from him. He had no one. He was helpless.

Barry was utterly and completely alone.

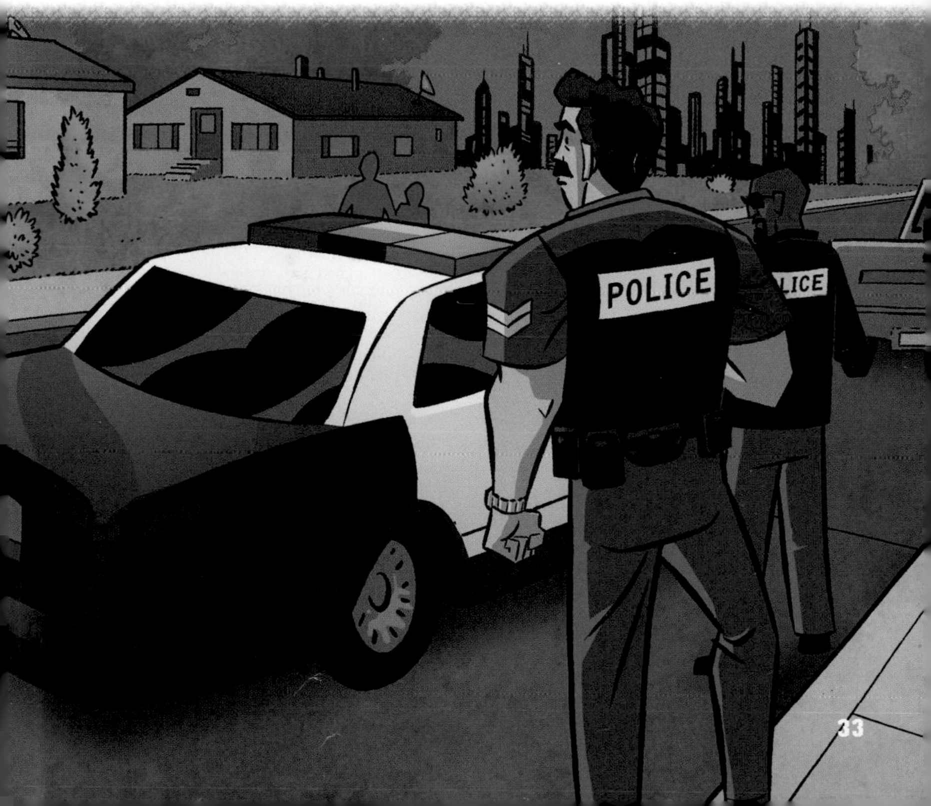
POLICE
LICE

But Barry wasn't one to give up. He used his father's case as inspiration. He studied hard in school and grew into a young man with a mission. He would find a way to clear his father's name.

He trained his mind to become a police forensic scientist. He spent nights at the office and worked through weekends on dozens of occasions.

On the sunniest days and the stormiest nights, Barry studied every piece of evidence related to his mother's death. He looked for any clues that would set his father free. Although working alone, he was determined to prove his father was innocent. No matter if the process went slowly or as quick as . . .

. . . a bolt of lightning.

CHAPTER 4

A Change In The Forecast

The mixture of chemicals and electricity gave Barry Allen the super-speed powers of The Flash that night. And although he may now be alone once again as he faces the Rogues, he is far from helpless.

The Flash grits his teeth and begins to run.

The Flash has defeated each of these Rogues before, but never all at once.

"I'll have to move even faster than normal if I'm going to pull something off," The Flash says as he zig-zags toward Captain Cold.

WHOOSH!

Captain Cold isn't sure how he is suddenly whisked away to Central Stadium, but he has a good idea.

"This will stop you —" He raises his cold gun and fires before he can finish his latest cringe-worthy pun. But the icy blast doesn't find its target. The Flash zooms away at a speed even Cold hasn't witnessed before. Of course, it's too late for Captain Cold to stop himself now. He has already pulled the trigger.

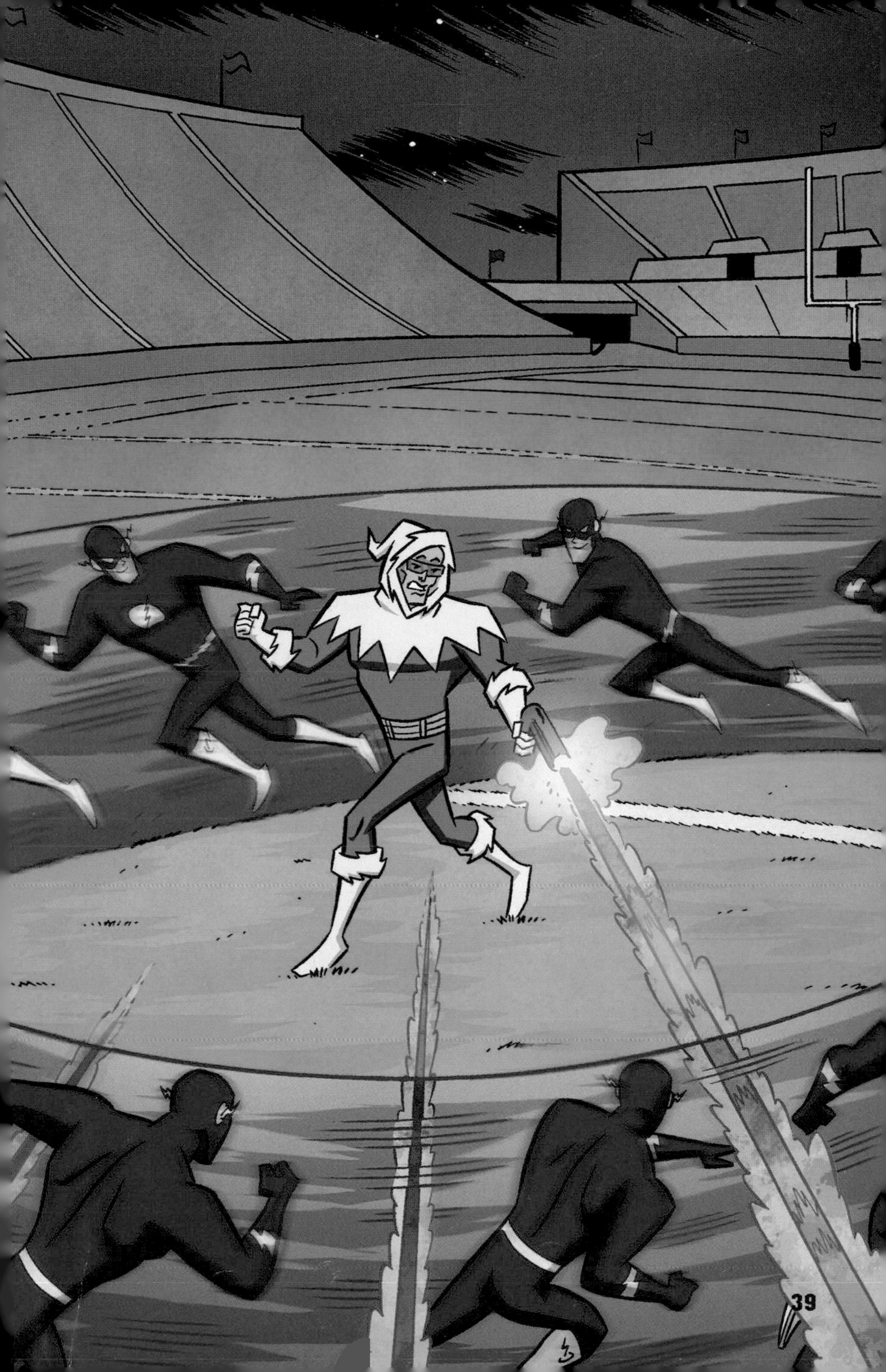

KRINNG! The blast shoots across the empty field.

Out of nowhere, a target appears. The icy ray strikes . . . Heat Wave?

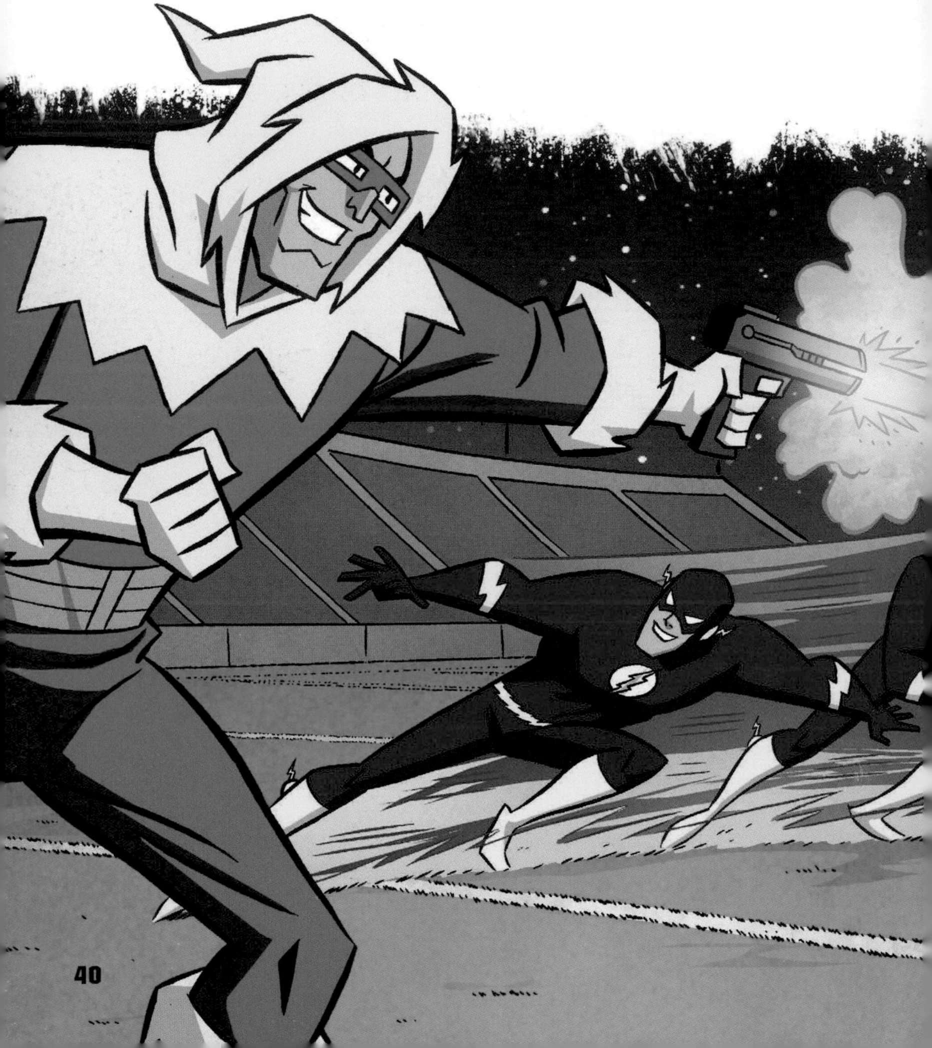

"— cold!" Captain Cold says, finally finishing his sentence.

"Wh-what!? How did I g-get here?" Heat Wave asks through chattering teeth.

"Just hang tight, hot shot," The Flash replies before he speeds out of the stadium.

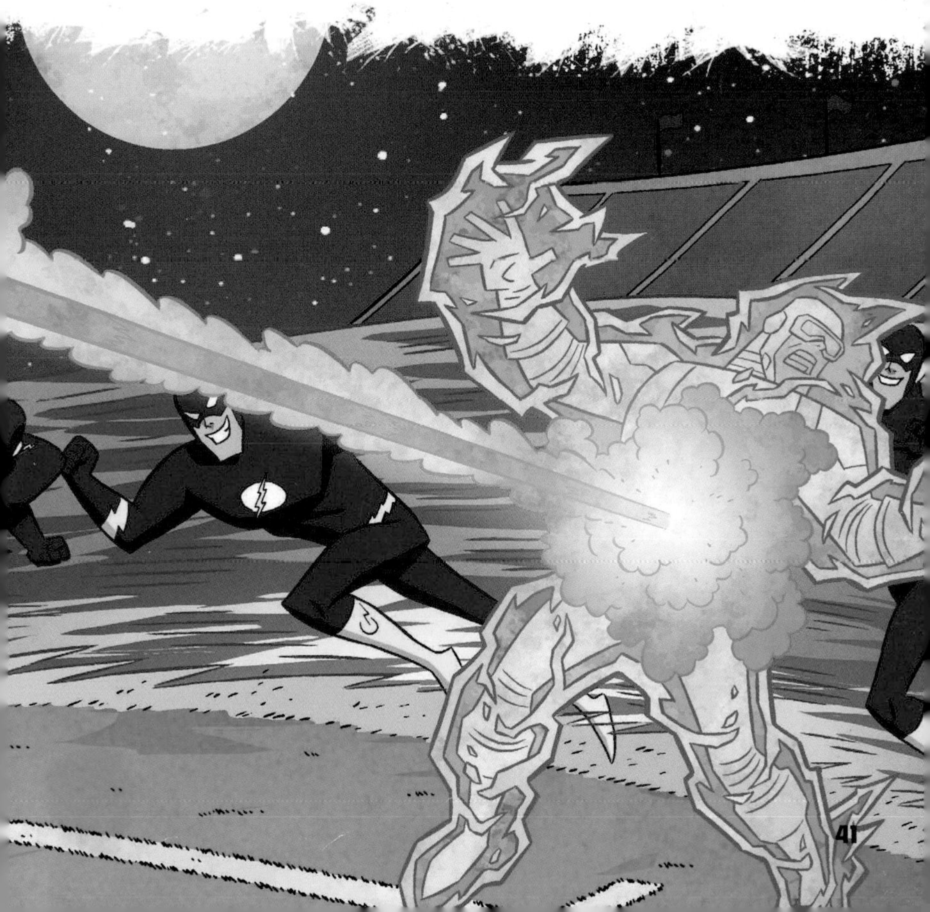

As The Flash drops Weather Wizard in the center of the stadium, the villain is quick to send a bolt of lightning careening towards the hero.

"Hands off, Flash!" Weather Wizard shouts at the red streak. But the hero doesn't wait around to hear the villain's speech echo in the nearly empty arena.

The lightning sails towards the Mirror Master, who suddenly finds himself across the lawn from the Weather Wizard. The Mirror Master is just as surprised as anyone when the bolt of electricity bounces off his handheld mirror . . .

PWING!

. . . and strikes the Weather Wizard down instead.

The Flash darts past the confused Mirror Master just as Captain Cold fires at him once more. Mirror Master is frozen solid in an instant. His mirror shatters from the extreme temperature.

KRASSH!

"Haha, you guys crack me up," says The Flash with a smile.

Captain Cold doesn't have time to reply. Before he can even open his mouth, he feels something like a freight train collide with his jaw.

The Flash had delivered each of his enemies to the stadium, pitting them against one another. And then he delivers the devastating knock out finale.

POW!

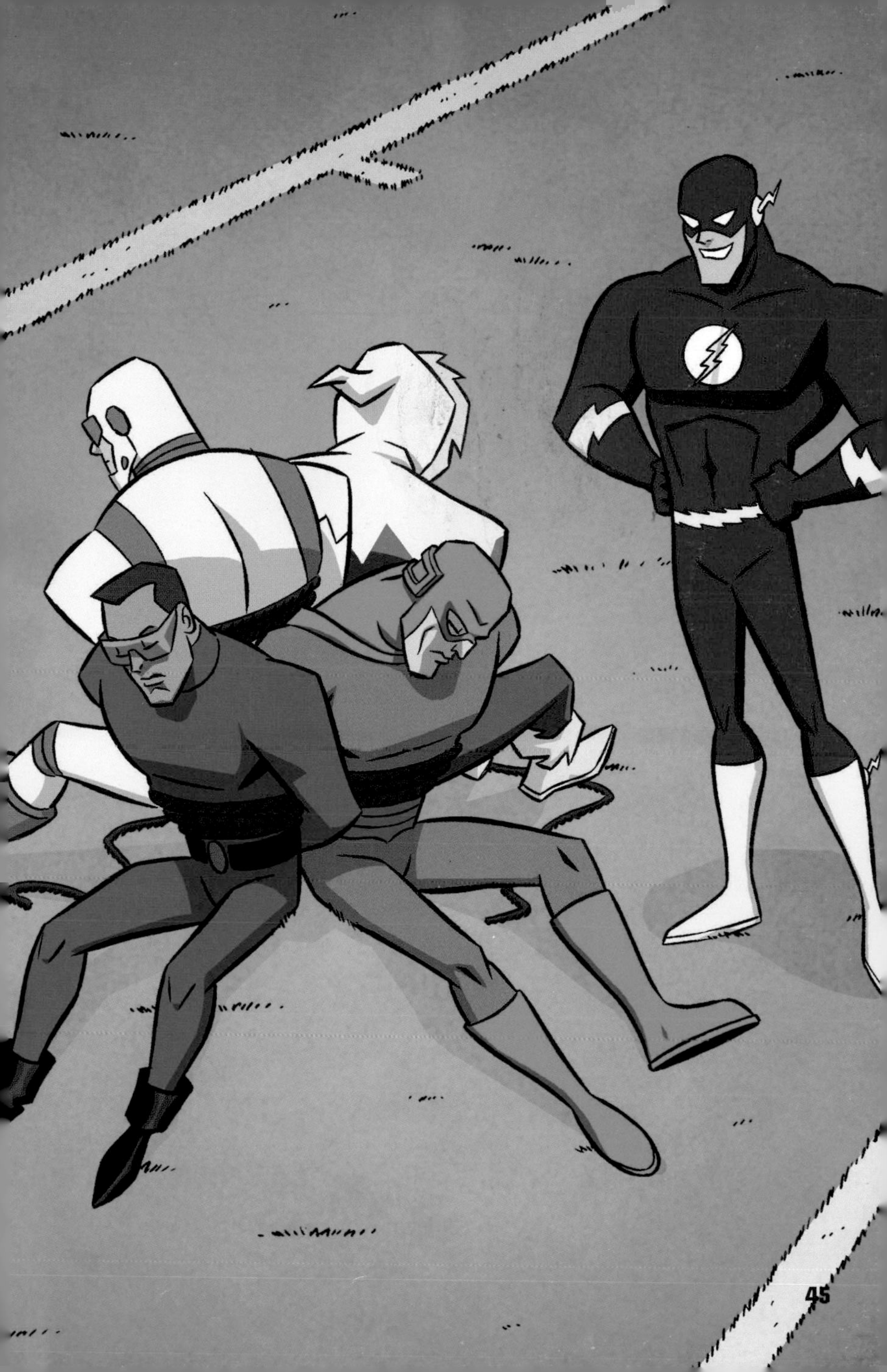

As The Flash binds his four unconscious enemies, he hears a voice in his cowl radio.

"This is Green Lantern," the voice says. "You still need help, Barry?"

The radio crackles as if in response.

"Nope," The Flash says. "The party is over."

WHOOSH!

He feels the wind rush against his face as he runs.

BOOM!

He hears the sound barrier thunder behind him. And once again, Barry Allen smiles.

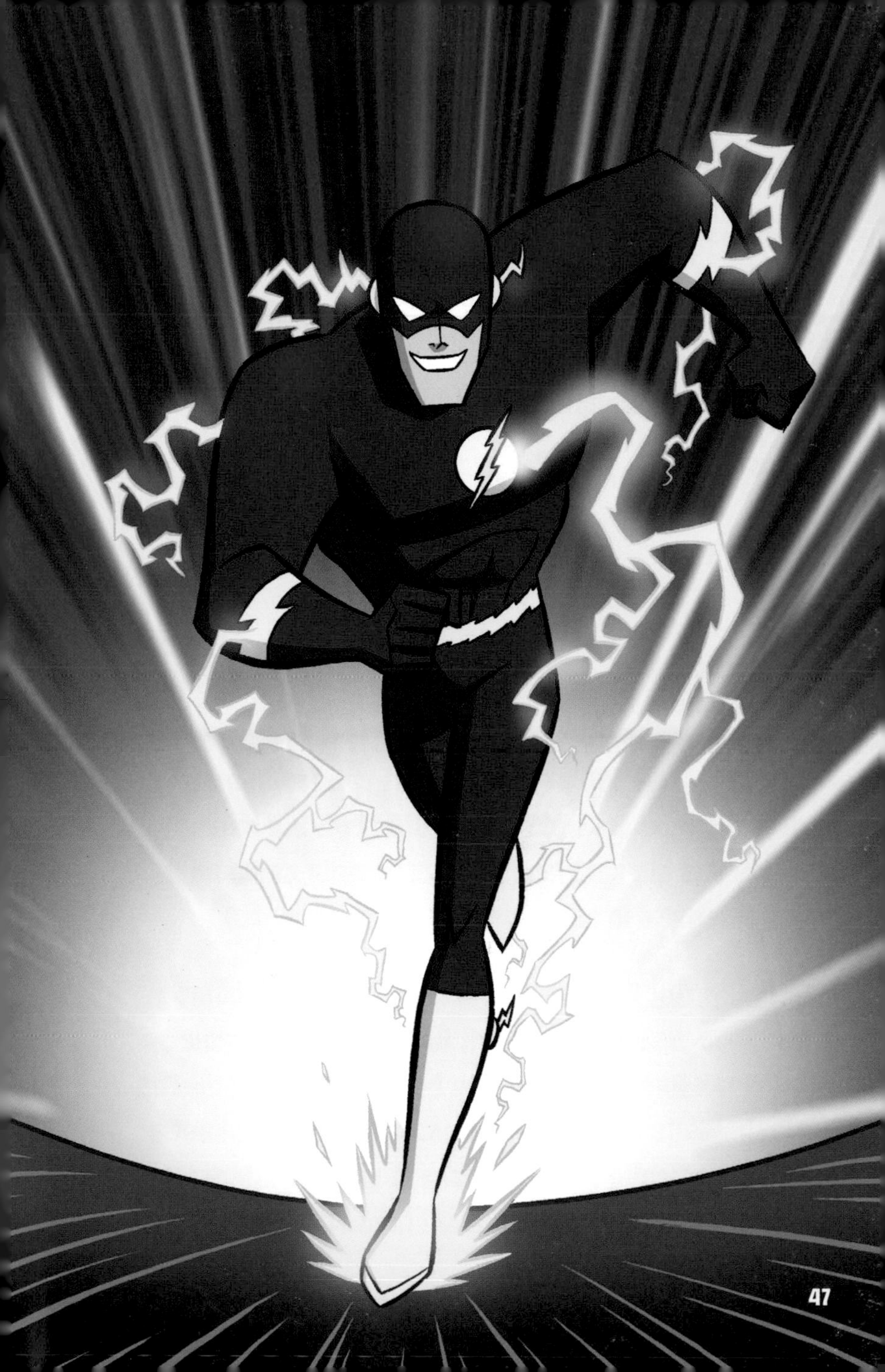

THE ROGUES

ALTER EGO: Captain Cold

REAL NAME: Leonard Snart

ROLE: Professional criminal

BASE: Central City

HEIGHT: 6' 2"

EYES: Brown

HAIR: Brown

ABILITIES: Wields a cold gun that can lower any object's temperature to absolute zero. His nerves of ice and his cold heart let him remain cool and collected. He is also a skilled marksman.

BACKGROUND: Leonard Snart ran away from home when he was a young man. He set out to become a criminal. During his first job he was captured by The Flash. While Snart was in prison he learned about a technologically advanced freeze gun. He later stole the cold gun and began to call himself Captain Cold.

ALTER EGO: Heat Wave

REAL NAME: Mick Rory

ROLE: Professional criminal

BASE: Central City

HEIGHT: 5' 11"

EYES: Blue

HAIR: Bald

ABILITIES: Can withstand high heat with a flame resistant suit that was covered and created with asbestos. Possesses a small flamethrower and knowledge of fire and explosives.

BACKGROUND: As a child, Mick Rory set fire to his house. He ran away from home and joined the circus. He eventually set fire to that too. Rory realized his obsession would serve him well as a super-villain. The hot-headed, cold-hearted criminal has run wild ever since.

ALTER EGO: Weather Wizard

REAL NAME: Mark Mardon

ROLE: Professional criminal

BASE: Central City

HEIGHT: 6' 1"

EYES: Blue

HAIR: Black

ABILITIES: Can control the weather with his weather wand. Possesses limited magnetic manipulation.

BACKGROUND: One night, while running from the police, Mark Mardon hid out at his brother's house. His brother, a brilliant scientist, had just built a device to control Earth's weather. That night, the siblings fought and Mardon's brother died. No one knows if the death was accidental. Mardon stole the weather wand and ran away. He now uses the wand to continue his life of crime.

ALTER EGO: Mirror Master

REAL NAME: Evan McCulloch

ROLE: Professional criminal

BASE: Central City

HEIGHT: 5' 11"

EYES: Brown

HAIR: Brown

ABILITIES: Maintains a collection of reflective weapons. Can turn an enemy's reflection against them, trap opponents in mirrors, and transport himself from one mirror to another.

BACKGROUND: Evan McCulloch was bullied as a child. He eventually turned to a life of crime. His shady skills caught the attention of the United States government. They wanted him to work for good instead of evil. But McCulloch was stuck in his corrupt ways.

GLOSSARY

careen (kuh-REEN)—to go forward quickly without control

collide (kuh-LYD)—to crash together forcefully, often at high speed

evidence (EV-uh-duhnss)—information, items, and facts that help prove something to be true or false

foe (FOH)—an enemy

frequency (FREE-kwuhn-see)—the number of sound waves that pass a location in a certain amount of time

gale (GAYL)—a strong wind

gust (GUHST)—a sudden, strong blast of wind

shatter (SHAT-ur)—to break into tiny pieces

unconscious (uhn-KON-shuhs)—not awake; not able to see, feel, or think

About the Author

Matthew K. Manning is the author of over fifty books. He has contributed to many comic books as well, including *Teenage Mutant Ninja Turtles: Amazing Adventures*, *Beware the Batman*, and the crossover miniseries *Batman/TMNT Adventures*. He currently resides in Asheville, North Carolina, with his wife Dorothy and their two daughters, Lillian and Gwendolyn. Visit him online at www.matthewkmanning.com.

About the Illustrator

Ethen Beavers is a professional comic book artist from Modesto, California. His best-known works for DC Comics include *Justice League Unlimited* and *Legion of Superheroes in the 31st Century*. He has also illustrated for other top publishers, including Marvel, Dark Horse, and Abrams.

WRITING PROMPTS

1. The super-villains in this story each have a different power. If you could have one of their powers, which would you choose? What would you do with your new power?

2. Imagine you could run as fast as The Flash. Where would you go? What would you do? Write about having super-speed for a day.

3. Do you think The Flash will face these super-villains again? Write a story about what would happen if they met again.

DISCUSSION QUESTIONS

1. The Flash decides he needs help and calls for backup from his fellow super heroes. Who do you go to when you need help with something?

2. Which of the four super-villains in this story caused the most trouble for The Flash? Why?

3. This book uses illustrations to help tell the story. Which illustration do you think helps the reader understand the action the most? Why?

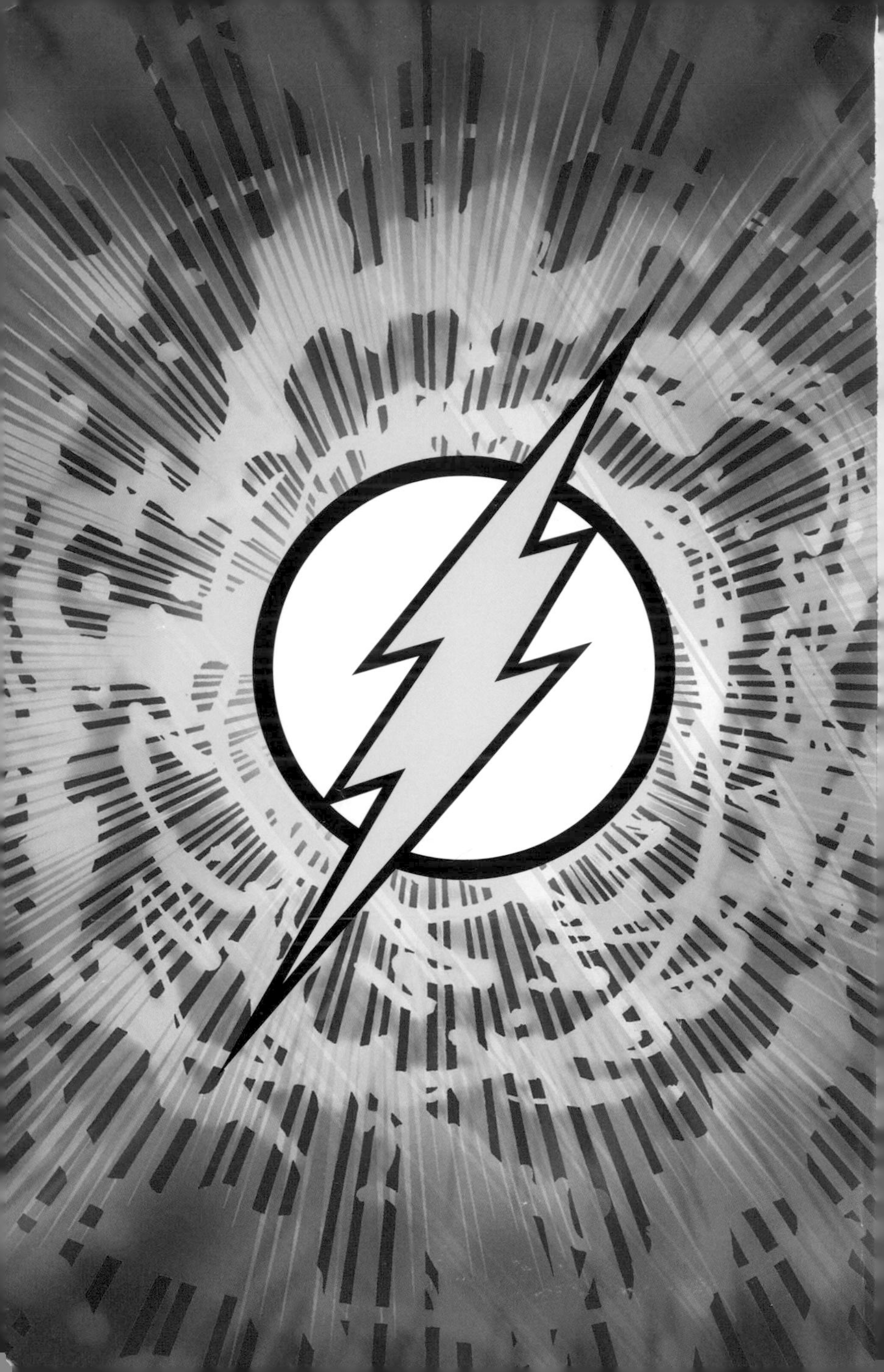